THE WOMAN WHO SAVED THINGS

Phyllis Krasilovsky • pictures by John Emil Cymerman

TAMBOURINE BOOKS NEW YORK

9/95'
with love from
Uncle Herb and
Aunt Laura

Text copyright © 1993 by Phyllis Krasilovsky
Illustrations copyright © 1993 by John Emil Cymerman

Library of Congress Cataloging in Publication Data
Krasilovsky, Phyllis. The woman who saved things/by Phyllis Krasilovsky:
pictures by John Emil Cymerman.—1st ed. p.cm.
Summary: Even though she doesn't always find a use for the things she
collects, an old woman continues to fill her house with interesting items.
[1. Collectors and collecting—Fiction. 2. Old age—Fiction.]
I. Cymerman, John Emil. ill. II. Title.
PZ7.K865Wo   1993 [E]—dc20   92-5126 CIP AC
ISBN 0-688-11162-9—ISBN 0-688-11163-7 (lib. ed.)
10 9 8 7 6 5 4 3 2 1
First edition

For Jessica Anne Krasilovsky,
an extraordinary collector

P. K.

For Lynn, my wife and friend

J.E.C.

There once was a woman who lived with her cat in a little house. Her children and grandchildren lived far away, so she had plenty of room.

At first, part of the house was completely empty. Spiderwebs in corners looked like decorations!

Then, little by little, the woman began to fill up the rooms.

She got lots of packages, and she saved
the stamps, wrapping paper, and string that
came with every one.

Every Wednesday morning she went for
long walks because that was trash collection
day. She'd find all kinds of things that people
put outside their homes.

One day she drove her pickup truck back for a sofa that was only missing one leg, plus an old stovepipe that reminded her of a sculpture she'd seen in a museum.

The woman could never pass up a bargain. Once she bought a box of yarn balls on sale. She told herself she would learn how to knit a sweater, but in the end her cat had the fun of playing with the yarn.

She picked up a Chinese kite without a
tail at the Salvation Army for just a quarter,
a pair of roller skates without their straps
for just a dime, and a pretty doll without
any hair for only a nickel.

She was always buying and finding books.
She couldn't resist them. Her bookcases
got so full that she had to stack books against
the walls.

It was amazing how many things piled up!
It would have been hard to count them all.

One morning, the woman's son wrote that he and his family were coming to visit. First she was excited. Then she began to worry. What could she do to make room for them? The guest beds were covered with things she'd collected. She decided to hold a sale.

She carried things down to her porch. She had to make many trips. It was hard to decide what prices to charge for the stuff she'd collected. She'd forgotten all about things that suddenly seemed valuable.

"I really can't sell this box of string," she said to herself. "I'll need it to tie back the bushes.

"I really can't sell these yarn balls. The cat enjoys playing with them." She put them back inside as well.

And so it went. She began to feel tired, so she lay down on the three-legged sofa. Before long she fell asleep.

When she woke up, her son and his family were there. "I'm happy you're here," she said, "but everything is quite a mess. I was planning a porch sale to get rid of things so you'd have more room."

"What fun!" they said. "We'll help you!"
And they did.

There were some things left over. Her grandson asked for the strapless skates to make skateboards for himself and his sister.

Her son was happy to take home a lot of the books she'd finished reading.

Her daughter-in-law loved the idea of using the old stovepipe as a sculpture on her lawn.

Her granddaughter asked for some yellow yarn to make a wig for the doll and to put a tail on the Chinese kite.

The woman and her grandchildren had plenty of string to make the kite fly higher and higher.

The woman was happy that everyone had found something to enjoy and that she wouldn't have to fix everything up herself!

The morning they left, they tied the stovepipe to the car roof so it wouldn't fall off. "It's a good thing I saved that heavy string," the woman said. "I always knew it would come in handy for something!"

After they were gone, she used the rest of it to tie the bushes against the house.

She propped the sofa with old books and plopped down on it to think about the pleasant visit. It was a relief not to have so many things around. She was glad her saving days were over.

Then she decided to go for a walk. She'd forgotten it was Wednesday, trash collection day, so she was surprised to see a lot of interesting things along the roadside. She walked right past them though. "I won't bother to look at what's out there," she said. "After all, my collecting days are over."

But then her eye was caught by the legs of an ironing board. It wouldn't hurt to get a closer look. "That board's in great shape," she thought. "It could make a good table for plants." But she left it there.

A little further on she saw a bathtub with claw legs. "That could make a great garden pool," she thought. "I could sink it into the ground and put goldfish in it. Maybe a couple of water lilies, too." But she walked on.

She saw an old vase that could make a nice lamp, and a broken-masted sailboat that could float in the bathtub.

There was an old record player that would be handy for spinning clay pots, and a bookcase that only needed one new shelf.

Then she spied a dressmaker's dummy that would be perfect for scaring the birds out of her vegetable garden.

Without another thought she raced home for her truck so she could beat the trash collector.

She had to make several stops to pick up the vase, the phonograph, the ironing board, the bookcase, and several other things.

Luckily, the trash collector came along just as she was wondering how to lift the bathtub.

He offered to deliver it to her. "You'll save me the trouble of hauling this heavy old thing to the dump," he said.

After everything was unloaded the woman realized she was right back where she'd started, saving things again. But never mind. That's what she liked to do best! Now if only she weren't feeling too lazy to dig the hole for the bathtub, fix the shelf for the bookcase, and fix the mast on the boat, she'd be all set.

Well, maybe she'd do it tomorrow. In the meantime, she put one of her old hats on the dressmaker's dummy in her vegetable garden.